Johnny Appleseed

Bruce Isham

illustrations

Marion & Steve Isham

Johnny was a hero
Everywhere he went
Some folks that he stayed with
Said he was heaven-sent
He always had a lot of friends
He was known quite well by all
And Johnny loved the children
The big ones and the small

NATHANIEL CHAPMAN

CARPENTER

The animals of the forest
Were Johnny's friends as well
Of squirrels and the bear cubs
Great stories he would tell
When they saw him coming down the path
They didn't run away
They knew it was Johnny Appleseed
So they stayed around to play

The Indians and the pioneers
Enjoyed it when he came
He always brought some appleseeds
That's how he got his name
He helped them plant their orchards
He helped them build their farms
And many trees from the forest
Were cut with his mighty arms

Johnny sometimes dressed real strange
Never cared much how he looked
And he would often sit alone
Beside a quiet brook
In the forest he felt right at home
And through the grassy plains he'd roam
Wherever apple trees would bloom
He knew there'd always be some room

Mostly Johnny walked alone
Sometimes a friend he took
But you would never find him
Without his precious books
He often read the Bible
He talked to God each day
It was others he had on his mind
When he bowed his head to pray

Johnny was a hero
Everywhere he went
He kept on traveling far and wide
Till he was grey and bent
He gave to those who had a need
Then he'd plant for them an apple tree
He's the kind of friend
We all should be

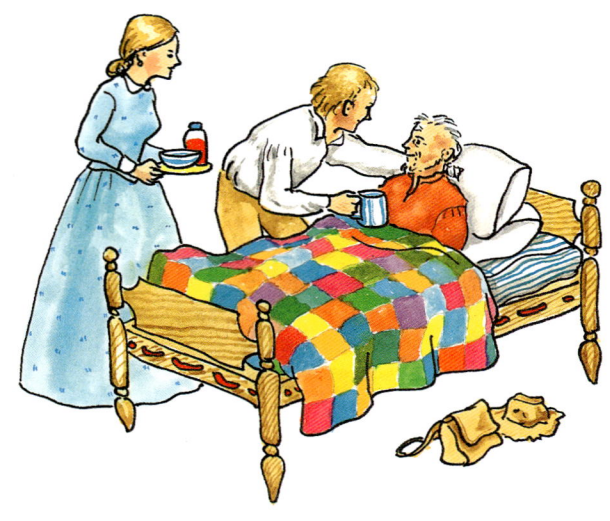

Johnny Appleseed

Johnny was a hero
Everywhere he went
Some folks that he stayed with
Said he was heaven-sent
He always had a lot of friends
He was known quite well by all
And Johnny loved the children
The big ones and the small

The animals of the forest
Were Johnny's friends as well
Of squirrels and the bear cubs
Great stories he would tell
When they saw him coming down the path
They didn't run away
They knew it was Johnny Appleseed
So they stayed around to play

The Indians and the pioneers
Enjoyed it when he came
He always brought some appleseeds
That's how he got his name
He helped them plant their orchards
He helped them build their farms
And many trees from the forest
Were cut with his mighty arms

Johnny sometimes dressed real strange
Never cared much how he looked
And he would often sit alone
Beside a quiet brook
In the forest he felt right at home
And through the grassy plains he'd roam
Wherever apple trees would bloom
He knew there'd always be some room

Mostly Johnny walked alone
Sometimes a friend he took
But you would never find him
Without his precious books
He often read the Bible
He talked to God each day
It was others he had on his mind
When he bowed his head to pray

Johnny was a hero
Everywhere he went
He kept on traveling far and wide
Till he was grey and bent
He gave to those who had a need
Then he'd plant for them an apple tree
He's the kind of friend
We all should be

Notes

Inside covers: there are hundreds of apple varieties growing in different countries; these are just 16 of them.

Inside the back cover: Folklore about apples: Isaac Newton - in 1666 Newton saw an apple fall from a tree. This led to his thoughts on the laws of gravity. William Tell - he refused to salute the cap of the bailiff Gessler and for this act of independence was sentenced to shoot with bow and arrow an apple on his son's head. Atalanta's Race - Atalanta refused to marry unless the suitor defeated her in a race. Milanion outran her by dropping 3 golden apples which she stopped to pick up. Snowhite and the 7 dwarves - Snowhite ate a poisoned apple given to her by the jealous queen. An apple for the teacher - a gift for the teacher. Upset the applecart - to spoil carefully made plans. The apple of my eye - very precious or much loved person or thing. An apple a day keeps the doctor away - healthy advice.

Page 4: these are places that Johnny Appleseed is known to have lived in or traveled through.

Page 5: Johnny Appleseed knew about herbal remedies and had a reputation as a healer among the settlers and Native Americans.

Children's games of the 18th and 19th centuries.

Page 6: animals that Johnny Appleseed may have encountered on his journeys.

Page 7: (North American birds from top left clockwise) Baltimore Oriole, Cedar Waxwing, Common Bluebird, Mockingbird, House Wren, Robin, Loggerhead Shrike, Yellow Warbler, Screech Owl, Yellowbilled Cuckoo, Common Nighthawk, Least Flycatcher, Barn Swallow, Crow, Blue Jay, Purple Martin, Horned Lark, Redheaded Woodpecker, Pigeon, Ringnecked Pheasant, Bald Eagle, Turkey, Herring Gull, Sparrow Hawk, Spotted Sandpiper, Snow Goose, Bobwhite, Killdeer, American Coot, Merganser, American Goldfinch, Common Meadowlark, Cardinal, Common Egret, Green Heron, Mallard, Common Snipe.

Page 8: Native American tribes of the North East.

Page 9: the four seasons.

Page 10: silverbirch, oak, beech, chestnut, ash, pine.

Page 11: North American fish.

Page 12 and 13: Lewis and Clark and Sacajawea, Pony Express, Crazy Horse, Davy Crockett, Pecos Bill, John Henry, coyote howling at the moon, Oregon Trail, Paul Bunyan and his ox Babe, Gold digger, Jim Bridger, "Fur Traders on the Missouri" by George Caleb Bingham, Laura Ingalls and the little house in the big woods, Groundhog, Erie Canal, Hiawatha, Pocohantas, Jack o'lantern, Huckleberry Finn and Jim, Abe Lincoln, Brer Rabbit, Annie Oakley and Buffalo Bill, Little Women, George Washington and the cherry tree, "Last of the Mohicans", Uncle Sam,

Arkansas Traveler, Ben Franklin and his stove, Paul Revere, the first Thanksgiving, Daniel Boone, Edgar Allan Poe and the raven, Rip Van Winkle, Betsy Ross.
Page 14: Books that Johnny Appleseed may have read and had in his traveling library.
Page 15: An abecedary from an early chapbook, a cheap little book sold by a Chapman or trader. A apple pie, B big boy, C cook, D dandy, dainty table, E English flag, Englishman(John Bull), F French soldier, French flag, fleur de lis, G giant gardener, H harlequin, hat, hair, horse, I Iroquois, J John Hancock, Thomas Jefferson, K King, knot, L Lilliputian, ladder, M mourner, N nurse, O officer, P Puritan, Q quartermaster, R Betsy Ross, S Sons of Liberty, T first Thanksgiving, U Uncle Sam, V vagabond (Johnny Appleseed), W George Washington.
Page 16: Heroes.

There are 22 pictures of Johnny Appleseed in this book, including the one on this page. Can you find them all?

On page 4, Nathanial Chapman is making a wooden horse for his son John. He attached wheels to the base. There is a picture of this little wooden horse hidden somewhere in each of the large illustrations. There are 10 including the one on this page.

Bandicoot Books
PO Box 50
Margate Tasmania 7054
Australia

www.bandicootbooks.com

Johnny Appleseed was born John Chapman, the son of Nathaniel and Elizabeth Chapman on September 26, 1774 in Leominster, Massachusetts. On April 18, 1775 Paul Revere called the Minutemen to fight the War of Independence.
John went to school until he was 14 and then was hired out to local farmers and orchardists. In 1797 at the age of 23 he headed west. He collected apple seeds from the cider mills of Pennsylvania and planted apple tree nurseries. John described himself as "by occupation a gatherer and planter of apple seeds". He died after a fever on March 18, 1845 in Indiana, sixteen years before the American Civil War.

to my wife, Cindy (Cinderfoot) - B.I.

to the memory of dad, Richard Westerman, planter of trees - M.I.

National Library of Australia
Cataloguing-in-Publication entry
Isham, Bruce
Johnny Appleseed

ISBN 0 9586536 3 1

1. Appleseed, Johnny, 1774-1845 - Juvenile poetry.
2. Picture Books for Children
I. Isham, Marion. II. Isham, Stephen E. III. Title

A821.3

Bandicoot Books
PO Box 50
Margate Tasmania 7054
Australia
Copyright © Bruce Isham, 1998
Illustrations copyright © Steve and Marion Isham, 1998
Reprinted 2001, 2003, 2006

All rights reserved. Without limiting the rights under copyright reserved above, no part of this publication may be reproduced, stored in or introduced into a retrieval system, transmitted, in any form or by any means (electronic, mechanical, photocopying, recording or otherwise), without the prior permission of the publisher and of the copyright owner of this book.
Printed in Singapore